6/4N

Dear Beast #3

Someone Is Missing!

by DORI HILLESTAD BUTLER

illustrated by
KEVAN ATTEBERRY

HOLIDAY HOUSE · NEW YORK

For Ben —D.H.B.

To the indefatigably curious Lily —K.A.

Text copyright © 2021 by Dori Hillestad Butler   Illustrations copyright © 2021 by Kevan Atteberry   All Rights Reserved

HOLIDAY HOUSE is registered in the U.S. Patent and Trademark Office.   Printed and bound in May 2021 at Toppan Leefung, DongGuan, China.

The artwork was created digitally with Photoshop.   www.holidayhouse.com   First Edition   1 3 5 7 9 10 8 6 4 2

Library of Congress Cataloging-in-Publication Data   Names: Butler, Dori Hillestad, author. | Atteberry, Kevan, illustrator.

Title: Someone is missing! / by Dori Hillestad Butler; illustrated by Kevan Atteberry.   Description: First edition.

New York: Holiday House, [2021]   Series: Dear Beast; #3 | Audience: Ages 6–9. | Audience: Grades 2–3.

Summary: Through a series of letters, snobby cat Simon and good-natured dog Baxter team up—sort of— to find Andy's missing school pet

Louie, the leopard gecko.   Identifiers: LCCN 2020038399 | ISBN 9780823448555 (hardcover)   Subjects: CYAC: Cats—Fiction.

Dogs—Fiction. | Leopard geckos as pets—Fiction. | Letters—Fiction. | Humorous stories.   Classification: LCC PZ7.B9759 So 2021

DDC [Fic]—dc23   LC record available at https://lccn.loc.gov/2020038399   ISBN: 978-0-8234-4855-5 (hardcover)

CONTENTS

O N E
WHO IS LOUIE?

FROM THE DESK OF

Simon

Dear Beast,
   It has come to my attention that something is bothering Andy. He failed to clean my litter box when he got home this afternoon. He doesn't want to play get the dot. And tonight, he even forgot to feed me! Do you know what's bothering him? Whatever it is must have happened at your house. He was fine when he left my house two days ago.

   Please write back soon.

Sincerely,
SIMON

Dear Simen,

Ya, I know whut the problim is. But it didn't happin at my howse. It happind at skool!

With a sad tail,
Beast

FTS: Hay! Did you know that the wurd "know" has a silint K at the beginning??? That's so kool!!!!!

Simon

Dear Beast,

    Of course I knew that. I trust this means you will spell "know" correctly from now on? That has always been your second most annoying misspelling. Most annoying are the many ways you misspell MY name! Again, it's S-I-M-O-N. If you would simply read your letters before you send them, I'm sure you would catch many of your errors.

    Now, what happened at school?

Curiously,

SIMON

Dear Syman,
   You haven't hurd the nooz?
Louie is misssing!
   You can't expekt me to chek
my speling when our boy is so
up set! Andy's dad made me a
nise dinner, but I can't eat it. I
can't evin think abowt food when
Andy is up set! Can you?

                    With a sad tail and
                    an empty stomick,
                    Beast

Simon

Dear Beast,

I always expect you to use proper spelling. And of course I still think about food when Andy is upset. I don't ask for much, but I do expect two meals and a clean litter box every day. I don't know why humans have to let every little thing disrupt my routine.

Who is Louie? Why is Andy so upset that he's missing?

Sincerely,
SIMON

Dear Simun,

Louie is Andy's klass pet at skool. I don't know whut kind of pet he is. That is a mistery. But I hope sumwon finds him soon. Utherwise Andy mite be sad furever!

With a sad tail, an
empty stomick,
and a hevvy hart,
Beast

FROM THE DESK OF

Simon

Dear Beast,

   Louie is probably just a hamster. No big deal. Andy will get over it. In the meantime, I'll just hop up on the counter and see what I can find for dinner. I'm sure things will look better tomorrow.

Cordially,
SIMON

TWO
LET'S BE DEETEKTIVES!

Dear Simon,

    Things are NOT better today. Now Andy and Noah are in a fite! Noah wuz supozed to bring Louie home for the weekend, but he can't becuz Louie is still missing! Noah thinks Andy left Louie's door opin when he fed Louie and that's why thay are in a fite. Hay! I have an ideeya! Let's be deetektives and find Louie. Then Andy and Noah will be best frends agen and evrywon will be happy!

Happy Tails,

Beast

FTS: Reemembir? That meens fergot to say. If we find Louie, we will be heros and Edgar Allan Crow will put our pickchurs in the Dayly Crow!

FROM THE DESK OF

Simon

Dear Beast,

Being a detective is not as easy as you think it is. You must talk to witnesses, study the clues, and use your brain to solve the case. You are not good at those things. But I am. I have learned from the best—my personal hero, Sherlock Holmes! Rest assured, I will find Louie. You can take a nap.

With confidence,
SIMON

Dear Symen,
    I'm not tyred. I want to
be a deetektive, too! I want
to help Andy. I want to find
Louie!

            Luv and Liver Treats,
            Beast

FROM THE DESK OF

Simon

Dear Beast,

No.

Firmly,

SIMON

Dear Symen Bossy Paw2,
  Why not??? I know stuff that you don't know. I just fownd out that Louie is not a hampstir. He is a lepurd gecko! See? You didn't know that, did you? Now can I be a deetektive with you?

        Luv and Liver Treats,
        Beast

Simon

Dear Beast,

No, you cannot.

Regrets,

Simon

THREE
THE DAILY CROW

FROM THE DESK OF
Simon

Dear Cheeks,

I know you like to gather nuts near Lincoln School. Have you heard that Louie, the leopard gecko from Andy's class, is missing? Have you seen him? Do you know what happened to him?

Yours in investigation,

SIMON

Dear Simon,

It's true. The best nuts in town are found outside Lincoln School. And yes, I heard that Louie was missing, but all I know is what I read in the Daily Crow.

Best,
CHEEKS

The Daily Crow

LOUIE IS MISSING!
BY EDGAR ALLAN CROW

Louie, the leopard gecko, has disappeared. He escaped from his cage in room 7 sometime on Wednesday night. Reports are mixed on what happened.

A human child (i.e., Noah) claims that another human child (i.e., Andy) left Louie's cage door open. Sources from Castle Rock School report, "There's a hole in Louie's roof. He's gotten out at least three other times this year. We don't know where he goes. The human who cleans the floor always finds him and brings him back. But that human is on vacation this week, so someone else will have to find Louie this time."

Extra! Extra! Read all about it! For a price . . .

Simon

Dear Edgar Allan Crow,

I am writing to report a mistake in your newspaper. You mentioned sources from Castle Rock School, but it's Lincoln School.

Also, you should have mentioned me in your article. I am the detective who will solve this case. I will find Louie.

Yours,

SIMON

Dear Simon,

Castle Rock School is correct. It's a school that's located inside Lincoln School. A school of—well, you say you're a detective, so you figure it out. Here are two clues for you. (No charge!)

1) Castle Rock School is surrounded by water.

2) If anything fishy is going on in room 7, those tail flippers will know about it. They don't miss a thing!

Sorry I didn't mention you in the last Daily Crow. I'll mention you in the next one.

Signed,
EDGAR ALLAN CROW

Dear Simon,

Why did you tell Baxter he can't help find Louie? Blub . . . blub . . . The thing about helping is anyone can do it! Blub . . . blub . . .

By the way, you're not the only one Andy forgets to feed when he's upset! Blub . . . blub . . . It may be in our best interest if you, Baxter, and I all work together to find Louie. Blub . . . blub . . .

Your acquaintance,
Blub . . . blub . . .
BUBBLES

FROM THE DESK OF

Simon

Dear Bubbles,
    Thank you for your letter. I prefer to work alone.

                Respectfully yours,
                SIMON

FOUR

CASTLE ROCK SCHOOL

FROM THE DESK OF

Simon

Dear Castle Rock School,

I don't believe we've met. I am Simon the cat. Andy is my human.

I read about you in the Daily Crow. I am trying to find out what happened to Louie, the leopard gecko. Please tell me what you saw the night Louie disappeared. Don't leave anything out. Do you have any idea where Louie is now?

Yours in investigation,
SIMON

Blub . . .

Blub . . .

Dear Simon, *blub . . . blub . . .*

What an exciting week we've had! *Blub . . . blub . . .* First Louie escaped. Then we saw ourselves in the Daily Crow. And now we have a letter from you! *Blub . . . blub . . .*

We saw Louie escape through a small hole in his roof. *Blub . . . blub . . .* He was headed straight for us, so we all went to hide in the weeds. *Blub . . . blub . . .* When we came out, he was gone. *Blub . . . blub . . .* Frankly, we were relieved. *Blub . . . blub . . .* We don't know for sure where he went, but we have some ideas. *Blub . . . blub . . .* Moby thinks he's behind some books. *Blub . . . blub . . .* Coral thinks he's in the curtains. *Blub . . . blub . . .* Goldy thinks he's gone to a different classroom. *Blub . . . blub . . .* Wherever he is, we hope he is found soon! *Blub . . . blub . . .*

We would like to know what it's like where you live. Are there castles there? Or rocks? *Blub . . . blub . . .* Will you be our pen pal? *Blub . . . blub . . .*

From,
Your friends at Castle Rock School
Go, Guppies!

FROM THE DESK OF

Simon

Dear Castle Rock School,

    I am far too busy for pen pals. You might try Bubbles. She seems to have a lot of free time. Thank you for your kind reply.

Thoughtfully,
SIMON

Dear Simon,

My name is Muffet. I heard you're looking for Louie. I can tell you he's still inside room 7. I have 352 children and our web is right outside the classroom door. I haven't slept since he escaped his cage. Geckos eat spiders, so my eight eyes have been glued to that door. I am certain Louie has not left room 7.

Please find him. I'm worried for my children. It's so hard to keep them in the web.

Yours,

MUFFET

FROM THE DESK OF

Simon

Dear Muffet,

Thank you for your letter. Don't worry. I will find Louie. I am a very good detective.

Respectfully,
SIMON

Dear Simmin,

Hay! Did you know there's anuther skool inside Andy's skool? It's called Kassle Rock Skool. Thay just became pen pals with Bubbles. Thay want to help us find Louie. YAY! KASSLE ROCK SKOOL!

Thay sed there's a hole in Louie's roof and that's how Louie got owt. That meens it's not Andy's fawlt that Louie is misssing! I wish we cud tell Noah that. Then maybe Andy and Noah cud make up!

Luv and Liver Treats,
Beast

FROM THE DESK OF

Simon

Dear Beast,

    Of course, I know about Castle Rock School. I also know about the hole in Louie's roof. I am a detective. It's my job to know things. I will find Louie. Look for my picture in the Daily Crow.

Surely,
SIMON

FIVE

UNDERCOVER SNAIL

The Daily Crow

STILL MISSING!

BY EDGAR ALLAN CROW

Despite Simon the cat's best efforts, Louie remains at large. If you have any information about the missing gecko, please contact this reporter.

Blub . . .

Blub . . .

Dear Simon, *blub . . . blub . . .*

Guess what! We found a clue! *Blub . . .*
blub . . . Here it is. What do you think?
Blub . . . blub . . .

From,
Your friends at Castle Rock School
Go, Guppies!

FROM THE DESK OF
Simon

Dear Castle Rock School,

Please note that it is best to leave a clue where it is found. Everything that is around a clue provides just as much information as the clue itself. But since you have already removed it, let's see if it can still be of some use. Please tell me where it was found, when was it found, and who has touched it?

Thank you for your time.

Cordially,

SIMON

Blub . . .

Blub . . .

Dear Simon, *blub . . . blub . . .*

We are sorry. We didn't know we shouldn't move clues. *Blub . . . blub . . .* We just wanted to help. We saw the clue under Jun's chair, but we're not sure how it got there. *Blub . . . blub . . .* Coral says she saw Louie take it off. *Blub . . . blub . . .* But Jack says that can't be right because Louie is "way bigger" than that. If the clue came from Louie, it would be bigger, too. *Blub . . . blub . . .* Coral says it was bigger . . . until Louie ate part of it. *Blub . . . blub . . .* Do you think that could be true? *Blub . . . blub . . .*

We couldn't get to the clue ourselves, so we asked Snail for help. *Blub . . . blub . . .* We are pretty sure he's the only one who has touched it. *Blub . . . blub . . .*

We are worried about Andy. He hasn't gone outside for recess since Louie disappeared. *Blub . . . blub . . .* He just stares sadly into Louie's empty cage.

From,
Your friends at Castle Rock School
Go, Guppies!

FROM THE DESK OF
Simon

Dear Snail,

   I understand you picked up a clue in room 7. What can you tell me about it? One Castle Rock guppy says it came from Louie. Another says it didn't. How can we know for sure where it came from?

Carefully,
SIMON

Dear Simon,

   I know the clue came from Louie. But I cannot tell you how I know. Remember, I once worked as a spy. Would you like me to go back to room 7 and have another look around? I would do that. For you.

Undercover,
SNAIL

FROM THE DESK OF
Simon

Dear Snail,

   I would like that very much. In fact, if you could take some photos of room 7 while you're there, that would also be helpful.

   I've been reading about leopard geckos. I know they like warm, dark hiding places. Once I see your photos, I'll be able to figure out where Louie is!

Confidently,
SIMON

Dear Simon,
    You can count on me!

                        Undercover,
                        SNAIL

SIX

BE PATIENT

Dear Simin,

Me and Bubbles hurd there was a klew, but we havin't seen it. Can you pleeze send it over? Also, why is Edgar Allan Crow deelivering the mail? Where is Snail?

Luv and Liver Treats,
Beast

Simon

Dear Beast,

    We don't want anything to happen to the clue, so I will hang on to it.

    Snail will be back soon. He's on a special assignment.

Mysteriously,

SIMON

Dear Simone,

    Whut kind of speshul assinement? Is it abowt Louie?

    Bubbles thinks I shud break owt of our backyard, go to Linkin Skool and surch for more klews. I have a vary good noze, in kase you didn't know. Whut do you think? I kind of want to do it, but I don't want to get in trubble. . . .

Luv and Liver Treats,
Beast

Simon

Dear Beast,
    That is a terrible idea. You could get in a lot of trouble. Big trouble! Dog catcher trouble! Think about it.

Thoughtfully
SIMON

Dear Simmon,

DOG KETCHER TRUBBLE???? Yikes!!!
That wood be vary, vary bad!!!

I don't know whut to do. We have
to find Louie. Last nite, Andy opinned
his piggy bank and cownted his munny.
He wants to buy his klass a new pet
cuz he still thinks it's his fawlt Louie is
missing.

                    With a skaird tail,
                    Beast

FROM THE DESK OF

Simon

Dear Beast,

Don't worry. Andy will not need to purchase a new class pet. I am very close to finding Louie. Please be patient for just a little bit longer.

Helpfully,
SIMON

Where is that snail?

SEVEN
WURRIED

Dear Simmon,

Bubbles and I are vary, vary wurried. We're wurried abowt Andy. We're wurried abowt Louie. And we're reelly wurried about Snail! He's been gone a long time. We think he mite be missing now, too!!!

Bubbles can't leeve her bowl. You don't like to leeve your howse. I may have to take a deep breth and break owt of my yard. Snail cud be in reel trubble! And I may be the only one who can reskue him.

Bravely,

Beast

Simon

Dear Beast,

DO NOT BREAK OUT OF YOUR YARD! Snail is fine. Everyone is fine. I have collected many clues. I will put them together and solve this case. I will find Louie and I will find Snail. And I will do it without ever leaving my house.

Intelligently,
SIMON

Dear Simun,

How?

With a wurried tail,

Beast

The Daily Crow

SNAIL IS MISSING!
BY EDGAR ALLAN CROW

Word is out! Snail is not just a mail carrier. He is also a spy! This reporter has learned that Snail was sent on a secret mission to room 7. Unfortunately, Snail's cover has been blown. Reports from Castle Rock School claim that Snail has gone into hiding, but he hasn't been seen or heard from in a very long time. If you have information on where Snail could be, please contact this reporter.

Blub . . .

Blub . . .

Dear Simon,

Are you out of your mind? *Blub . . . blub . . .* You sent Snail to find Louie?!?! *Blub . . . blub . . .* Don't you know geckos EAT snails?

Definitely not your friend,
Blub . . . blub . . .
BUBBLES

FROM THE DESK OF
Simon

Dear Bubbles,

What makes you think I "sent" Snail anywhere? For your information, Snail offered to go to Lincoln School. He's a very good spy. I'm not worried.

Hopefully,
SIMON

Blub . . .

Blub . . .

Dear Simon,
  I know it was you! And I am not happy with you!

                    Blub . . . blub . . .
                    BUBBLES

Dear Simin,
I will find Snail! Maybee I'll find Louie, too!!! I am reddy to be a hero!!! Here I go!!!

Luv and Liver Treats,
Beast

EIGHT
NOT COMING HOME

FROM THE DESK OF

Simon

Dear Beast,
    What do you mean you are ready to be a hero? Where are you going? What are you doing?

Seriously,
SIMON

Blub . . .

Blub . . .

Dear Simon,
  Baxter isn't here. *Blub . . . blub . . .* He's out looking for Snail. And Louie. *Blub . . . blub . . .* He should have been back by now. *Blub . . . blub . . .*

                    With frightened fins,
                    Blub . . . blub . . .
                    BUBBLES

Simon

Dear Castle Rock School,

What is happening? When did you last see Snail? I understand he went into hiding. Do you know where? Is Baxter there with you?

Yours in investigation,
SIMON

Dear Simon, *blub . . . blub . . .*

    We had not seen Snail in quite a while. *Blub . . . blub . . .* But we see him now. *Blub . . . blub . . .* We see Louie, too. *Blub . . . blub . . .* We cannot bear to watch.

        From,

        Your friends at Castle Rock School

        Go, Guppies!

P. S. We've never met Baxter. Or seen a picture of him. So we don't know if he's here. *Blub . . . blub . . .*

Simon

Dear Castle Rock School,
   Tell me what is happening! I demand to know!

                    Furiously,
                    SIMON

Dear Simon, *blub . . . blub . . .*

Wow, what a day! We've been talking to Edgar Allan Crow for hours! *Blub . . . blub . . .* And now we're too tired to talk anymore. *Blub . . . blub . . .* If you want to know what happened, read tomorrow's Daily Crow. *Blub . . . blub . . .*

From,
Your friends at Castle Rock School
Go, Guppies!

Dear Simon,

   I am writing to inform you that Andy will not be returning to your home this evening. *Blub . . . blub . . .* After all that's happened, who can blame him? He just wants to cuddle with Baxter. *Blub . . . blub . . .* If I could leave this bowl, I'd cuddle up with the two of them, too. *Blub . . . blub . . .* Baxter is so brave! *Blub . . . blub . . .* Have a good night!

   Maybe your friend again someday,
   Blub . . . blub . . .
   BUBBLES

NINE
CASE CLOSED

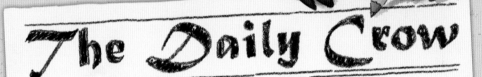

The Daily Crow

LOUIE IS HOME!
BY EDGAR ALLAN CROW

Thanks to the efforts of one brave hero who does not wish to be named, Louie the leopard gecko is back in his cage. Students from Castle Rock School report, "[Nameless Hero] discovered Louie hiding under a small refrigerator. He lured Louie out, led him back to his cage, and slammed the door!"

When asked why he would go to such trouble, our hero replied, "Someone had to do it."

"We're glad Louie is back home and we hope he'll stay there," says Muffet. "But someone needs to fix that hole in his roof. For good!"

When asked for a quote, the gecko replied, "No comment."

Dear Simon,

YAY!!! Louie is back home. Snail is safe. And gess whut else? Andy and Noah made up. Noah took Louie home today since he didn't get to do that last weekend.

Here's a pickchur of me and Andy and Noah and Louie!

Luv and Liver Treats,

Beast

Simon

Dear Beast,

  Tell me what happened. How did you know where Louie was hiding? How did you get him back to his cage?

Seriously,

Simon

Dear Siman,

Wait a minit. You think I'm the nameliss hero in the Dayly Crow? That's funny. I thawt that wuz you!

I never made it to Linkin Skool. I got cawt by the dog ketcher. It was vary, vary skairy at first. She put me in a kage all by myself. But then she came back and shined sumthing on my neck. It told her who my peeple are. So then she gave me ise creem and took me home. YAY! HOME!!!!

Luv and Liver Treats,
Beast

FTS: If I'm not the hero and yor not the hero, who is???

FROM THE DESK OF
Simon

Dear Beast,

   Well, I'm sure we can all agree that I am a hero even if I'm not the one who brought Louie home. I have just learned that Snail is the one who did that. I must say, I am more than a little bit impressed.

Sincerely,
SIMON

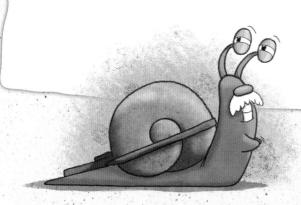

Dear Simon,

YAY! SNAIL!!!! I always noo he was a hero! I think we are all heros. YAY! US!!!

And hay! You were rite: you DID solv this kase without ever leeving your howse. You figyored that owt abowt Snail! I luv a happy ending. Don't you?

Luv and Liver Treats,
Beast

Simon

Dear Beast,

It's "knew," not "noo." I won't bother with the other twelve misspellings in your letter. But if you can spell "know," you should be able to spell "knew," too.

And of course I solved the case. I am a very good detective.

Yours,

Simon

DOGGY DICTIONARY

abowt = about

agen = again

anuther = another

assinement = assignment

becuz = because

breth = breath

cawt = caught

chek = check

cownted = counted

cud = could

cuz = because

dayly = daily

deelivering = delivering

deetektive = detective

evin = even

evrywon = everyone

expekt = expect

fawlt = fault

fergot = forgot

figyored = figured

fite = fight

fownd = found

frends = friends

FTS = Forgot to Say

furever = forever

gess = guess

hampstir = hamster

happin = happen

happind = happened

hart = heart

havin't = haven't

hay = hey

heros = heroes

hevvy = heavy

howse = house

hurd = heard

ideeya = idea

ise creem = ice cream

kage = cage

kase = case

kassle = castle

ketcher = catcher

klass = class

klew = clue

kool = cool

leeve = leave

leeving = leaving

lepurd = leopard

luv = love

maybee = maybe

meens = means

minit = minute

misssing = missing

mistery = mystery

mite = might

munny = money

nameliss = nameless

nise = nice

nite = night

noo = knew

nooz = news

noze = nose

opin = open

opinned = opened

owt = out

pawz = paws

peeple = people

pickchur = picture

pleeze = please

problim = problem

reddy = ready

reel = real

reelly = really

reemembir = remember

reskue = rescue

rite = write or right

sed = said

sez = says

shud = should

silint = silent

skaird = scared

skairy = scary

skool = school

solv = solve

speling = spelling

speshul = special

stomick = stomach

sumthing = something

sumwon = someone

supozed = supposed

surch = search

thawt = thought

thay = they

trubble = trouble

tyred = tired

up set = upset

utherwise = otherwise

vary = very

whut = what

wood = would

wurd = word

wurried = worried

wuz = was

ya = yeah